THE SPRING HAT

MADELAINE GILL

SIMON & SCHUSTER BOOKS FOR YOUNG READERS
Published by Simon & Schuster
New York   London   Toronto   Sydney   Tokyo   Singapore

To David

SIMON & SCHUSTER BOOKS FOR YOUNG READERS
Simon & Schuster Building, Rockefeller Center
1230 Avenue of the Americas, New York, New York 10020
Copyright © 1993 by Madelaine Gill
All rights reserved including the right of reproduction
in whole or in part in any form.
SIMON & SCHUSTER BOOKS FOR YOUNG READERS
is a trademark of Simon & Schuster.
Designed by Vicki Kalajian
Manufactured in the United States of America

10 9 8 7 6 5 4 3 2 1

Library of Congress Cataloging-in-Publication Data
Gill, Madelaine, The spring hat / by Madelaine Gill.
p. cm. Summary: Though Mother Bunny's children cause her
to lose her hat, they make it up to her very nicely.
[1. Hats—Fiction. 2. Rabbits—Fiction.] I. Title.
PZ7.G3988Sp 1992 [E]—dc20 91-30556 CIP
ISBN: 0-671-75666-4